FRIENDS FOREVER

The Adventures of
Melrose and Croc

by Emma Chichester Clark

HarperCollins *Children's Books*

Originally published individually as *Melrose and Croc – Friends for Life* and *Melrose and Croc – Find a Smile*
© Emma Chichester Clark 2006

This 2009 edition published by Barnes & Noble, Inc.,
by arrangement with HarperCollins Publishers Ltd, Great Britain.

HarperCollins Children's Books
77-85 Fulham Palace Road
London, W6 8JB
UNITED KINGDOM

978-1-4351-2254-3

Printed and bound in China
August 2009

1 3 5 7 9 10 8 6 4 2

Melrose and Croc

FRIENDS FOR LIFE

It was spring, and
a day for singing.
"I am green!" sang
Little Green Croc.

"And I am hairy," sang Melrose.

"I wish I were as clever as you!" said Melrose.

"I wish I were as clever as you!" said Little Green Croc.

"You can do somersaults!" said Little Green Croc.

"And you can draw airplanes!" said Melrose.

"But I wish you were as tidy as me!"
said Little Green Croc.

"Well, I wish you were as quiet as me!"
said Melrose.

"And I wish you weren't so greedy!"
said Melrose.

"Well, I wish you weren't so greedy!"
said Little Green Croc.

"I like the way you listen to me when I'm talking,"
said Little Green Croc.

"I like the way you help me when I need you,"
said Melrose.

"I wish I could sing like you!"
said Little Green Croc.

"I wish I could dance like you!"
said Melrose.

"I like the way you put the toothpaste on my toothbrush," said Little Green Croc.

"I like the way you brush your teeth!"
said Melrose.

"I wish I were more like you,"
said Little Green Croc.

"But you are you, and I am me..."
said Melrose,

"…you wouldn't be you if you were like me!
There's no one else in the world like you!"

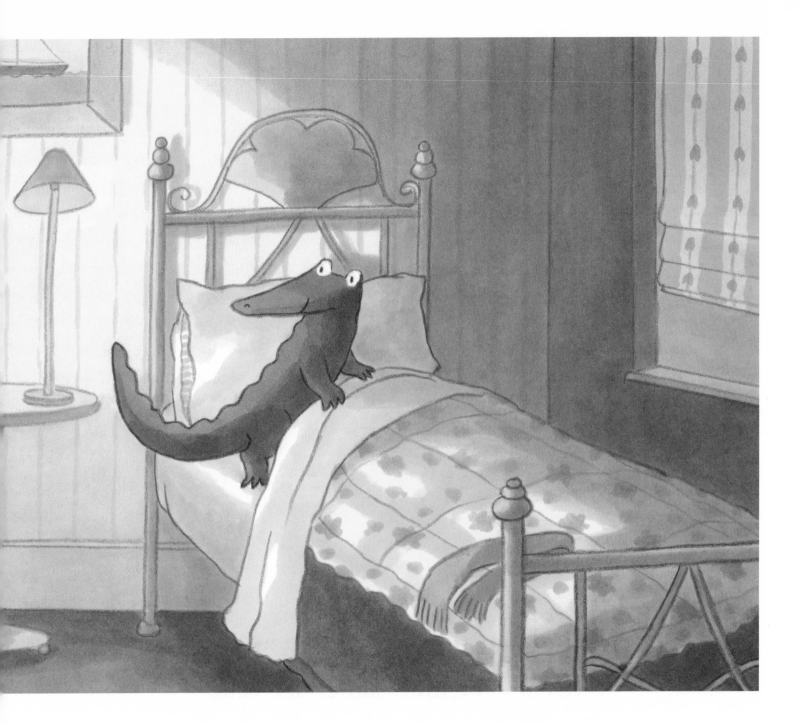

"No one like you and no one like me!"
sang Little Green Croc.

"I like us just the way we are...
friends for life!" sang Melrose.

Melrose and Croc

FIND A SMILE

It was a lovely sunny day,
but something was wrong.
"What's happened?"
asked Little Green Croc.

"I've lost my smile," said Melrose.

"Well, let's go and find it then!" said Little Green Croc.

Melrose and Little Green Croc got in the car
and drove out to the country.

"But how will we find it?" asked Melrose.

"Well," said Little Green Croc,

"first, we have to run, as fast as we can...

...just like this!"

"Then we have to hop over a stream,
without touching the water…

…just like this!" said Little Green Croc.

"Then we have to chase a squirrel up a tree,

just like this…

...and say hello to every cow,

just like this!" said Little Green Croc.

"Next, we find a yellow flower and smell it,"
said Little Green Croc, "just like this...

and catch a falling leaf, just like this...

...which you wear on your nose, just like this,

and walk backwards up the hill, just like this!"

said Little Green Croc.

"Then you sit in a special place and forget about everything," said Little Green Croc.

"What were we looking for?"
asked Little Green Croc.

"I can't remember!" said Melrose,
and he smiled, just like this!